THIS BOOK
BELONGS TO

. . . .

Every effort has been made to trace the ownership of all material. In the event of any question arising as to the use of the material, the publisher will be happy to make the necessary correction for use in future printings.

Stories retold by Gaby Goldsack and Kath Jewitt
Illustrations by Daniel Howarth and Steve Lavis

This edition published by Parragon in 2011

Parragon
Queen Street House
4 Queen Street
Bath BA1 1HE, UK

ISBN 978-1-4454-4652-3

Printed in China

MY TREASURY OF CLASSIC STORIES

PaRragon

Bath · New York · Singapore · Hong Kong · Cologne · Delhi
Melbourne · Amsterdam · Johannesburg · Auckland · Shenzhen

The Wind in the Willows illustrated by Daniel Howarth

···CONTENTS···

The River Bank

The Mole was fed up. "BOTHER spring cleaning!" he said, and, "BLOW spring cleaning!" He slammed the front door of his underground home behind him and raced up the tunnel that led to the open air.

"Up we go! Up we go!" he panted as he scratched and scraped to the surface until – POP – he found himself in the warm grass of a meadow. "Ah! This is better than whitewashing!" he said to himself as he skipped across the fields toward a river that rustled and swirled and glinted in the morning sun.

Mole had never seen a river before. He sat on the grass and gazed across the water.

"Hello!" called a voice from the bank on the other side of the river. A cheerful-looking creature with a round face, small neat ears, and thick silky fur was sipping lemonade on the terrace of his riverside home. It was the Water Rat.

"Hello, Ratty," said the Mole shyly.

"Hello Mr. Mole. Hang on and I'll come across in my boat," cried Ratty, stepping down into a little blue boat and rowing briskly across the river.

"I've never been in a boat before," said Mole nervously.

"What?" cried Ratty, as he put out a friendly paw to help Mole step into the boat.

"Is it nice?" asked the Mole.

"Nice? NICE? It's the ONLY thing," said the Water Rat. "Believe me, there is NOTHING – absolutely nothing – half so much worth doing as simply messing about in boats. I tell you what," he exclaimed. "Let's make a day of it. We'll have a picnic up the river. There's a hamper already packed under your seat!"

"What's in the basket?" asked the Mole.

"There's cold chicken," began Ratty, "coldhamcoldbeefcold pickledgherkinssaladFrenchrolls..."

"Oh stop, stop!" laughed the Mole. "It's all too much." And with that Ratty began to row steadily up the river.

The Mole sighed with contentment and leaned back into the soft cushions. "This is wonderful," he murmured.

"I like your black velvet suit,"
smiled Ratty after some half hour or so
had passed.

"I beg your pardon, I was daydreaming,"
said the Mole, pulling himself together with an effort
and looking around him. "What lies over THERE?"
he asked, waving a paw toward a wood on the far
bank of the river.

"Oh, that's the Wild Wood," said Ratty
shortly. "We river bankers don't go there if
we can help it."

"Why not?" asked Mole nervously.

"There are weasels and stoats in the
Wild Wood," said Ratty darkly, "you can't
trust them. And Badger, of course. Dear old
Badger. They'd better not interfere with
him, not with Badger."

"Ah, here's our picnic spot," said Ratty.

They picnicked on the green banks of a backwater, where the tumbling waters of a weir filled the air with a soothing murmur of sound.

"What are you looking at?" asked Ratty after a while.

"I am looking," said the Mole, "at a streak of bubbles that are traveling along the surface of the water."

Suddenly, a broad, glistening muzzle with white whiskers broke the surface of the water.

"Mr Otter!" cried Ratty. "Meet my friend Mr Mole."

"Pleased to meet you," said the Otter, shaking the water from his coat.

There was a rustling from behind them and a black-and-white animal with a stripy head shouldered its way through a hedge.

"Come on, old Badger!" cried Ratty.

"Humph! COMPANY!" grumbled Badger, and turned his back and disappeared.

"That's *just* like Badger," explained Ratty. "Simply hates society." Just then, a racing boat, with a short, round figure, splashing badly and rolling a good deal, flashed into view.

"There's Toad!" cried the Otter. Ratty stood up and called out. Toad waved and then carried on rowing.

"Oh dear, oh dear!" chuckled Ratty. "It looks like Toad's got a new hobby. Once it was sailing. Then he tired of that and took to punting, then it was houseboating and he said he was always going to live in a houseboat. And now it's a racing boat."

The Otter shook his head. "It won't last! Whatever Toad takes up he tires of it and then starts on something new. What about the time when…?"

Just then, a wandering mayfly swerved overhead and then settled onto the river. There was a swirl and a CLOOP and the mayfly disappeared. And so did Otter, leaving behind him a streak of bubbles on the surface of the river.

The picnic party came to an end and the afternoon sun was setting as Ratty skulled homeward in a dreamy mood, not paying much attention to the Mole. But the Mole was getting restless and presently he said, "Ratty! Please, I want to row now!" He jumped up and seized the oars, so suddenly that the Rat fell backward.

"Stop, you *silly* fool!" cried Ratty from the bottom of the boat. "You'll tip us over!"

The Mole made a great dig at the water with the oars, missed the surface altogether, found himself suddenly lying on top of the Rat, grabbed at the side of the boat, and the next moment – SPLOOSH – the boat capsized!

Oh dear, how cold the water was, and how *very* wet it felt!
The Mole felt himself sinking down, down, down.

How bright and welcome the sun looked as he rose to the surface, coughing and spluttering. How black his despair as he felt himself sinking again, until a firm paw grabbed him by the neck and he was pulled to the bank, a squashy, pulpy lump of misery.

"Now then, Mr. Mole, trot up and down the path until you're warm and dry again," instructed Ratty.

And so the sad Mole, wet and ashamed, trotted about until he was fairly dry. Meanwhile Ratty rescued the boat, the floating oars, and the cushions, before diving for the picnic basket.

It was a limp and sorry Mole, still a little wet on the outside and ashamed on the inside, that stepped into the boat. "Oh Ratty, can you ever forgive me for my stupidity? Shall we ever be friends again?"

"Goodness me, dear friend," laughed the good-natured Rat. "What's a little wet to a Water Rat? I'm more in the water than out of it most days. Don't you think any more about it, of course we will always be the best of friends. Look here, I really think you had better come and stay with me for a while and then I'll teach you to row and to swim and you'll soon be as handy on the water as any of us riverfolk."

The Mole brushed away a tear with the back of his paw and Ratty kindly looked in another direction.

When they got home, Ratty made a bright fire in the parlour, and found a bathrobe and slippers for the Mole to wear before seating him in a big armchair and telling him river bank stories until it was time for supper.

It was a very tired and contented Mole who was taken upstairs to the best bedroom, where he lay his head on a soft pillow and allowed the lap, lap, lap of the river to send him off to sleep. What a busy and wonderful day it had been.

The Golden Goose

Once there was a man who had three sons. Two of them were clever, but everybody thought the youngest, called Peter, was silly. Even his family made fun of him!

One day, the father sent the eldest son, Luke, into the forest to chop down a tree. He was his mother's favourite and she made him a tasty lunch of fruit cake and gave him a bottle of orange juice so he wouldn't go hungry or thirsty. He was just about to start work when a little old man appeared.

"Good morning, young sir," said the old man. "Please may I have a bit of your cake and a sip of your water? I'm hungry and thirsty." The eldest son shook his head.

"If I give you some, there won't be enough for me," Luke said. "Be off with you, old man." Then he turned his back on the old man and began to chop down the tree.

The old man shook his head sadly and disappeared.

CHIPPETY CHOP! OUCH! As if by magic, the eldest son's ax slipped and cut his arm, so he had to go home.

As Luke was unable to chop any more wood, the father sent his middle son, Paul, into the forest to chop down the tree. His mother also gave him some cake and a bottle of orange juice. Paul had not gone far when the old man appeared.

"Young sir, please will you share your food with me?" he asked. "I'm hungry and thirsty."

But the middle son wouldn't. "There will be none left for me," he laughed, ignoring the old man's strange expression. Then he lifted his ax to chop down the tree.

CHIPPETY CHOP! OOF! No sooner had Paul started work than his ax slipped and cut his leg, so he, too, had to go home.

"Father, will you let me chop down the tree?" asked Peter, when the middle brother limped home. His father laughed.

"Now that your older brothers have failed, what makes you think you can do it?"

Peter begged until, finally, his father gave in.

"Very well, Peter," he said. "If you hurt yourself, maybe it will teach you a lesson." Peter's mother went to prepare him some lunch but all she had left was some stale bread and a bottle of water. So Peter set off for the forest with his simple lunch and an ax.

It wasn't long before he met the little old man.

"Will you give me some of your lunch?" asked the old man. "I'm so hungry and thirsty."

Peter looked at his parcel of food.

"There's not much," he said. "But you are welcome to share it with me."

"You are a kind boy," said the old man, as they sat down to eat. "Let me give you something in return."

The old man told Peter to go over to an old tree and chop it down. "There is something special in its roots," he said mysteriously. Before Peter had a chance to ask what was under the tree, the old man had disappeared.

Peter did as the old man said and began to chop down the tree. When it fell, there in the roots of the tree was a goose with golden feathers. Peter had never seen anything so beautiful.

By now, it was getting late so Peter picked up the goose and went to find an inn to stay in for the night.

When Peter arrived at the inn people noticed his golden goose, including the innkeeper's three daughters. They gasped and crowded around the goose.

"What a beautiful creature!" they cried. Secretly, each girl decided to steal a golden feather.

That night, as Peter slept, the three girls crept up on the golden goose. One by one, they reached out to pluck a golden feather. But the moment they touched the bird, each found she was stuck to the goose and couldn't let go!

In the morning, the three girls were still stuck, but Peter took no notice of them. He just picked up his goose and set out for home – with the three girls trailing behind him.

A priest spotted the strange procession crossing the fields.

"Why are you running after this young man?" he cried. He took the youngest daughter by the hand to stop her. At once, the priest was stuck.

Just then, his assistant came along and tried to free the priest but, as soon as he touched him, he too was stuck. He couldn't let go no matter how hard he tried.

"Help us!" the priest's assistant called to some passing farm workers. "We're stuck!"

But as soon as the farm workers touched him, they were stuck, too. Now there were seven people running along behind Peter and his goose!

Soon Peter came to a city ruled by a king. His daughter was so sad that the king had offered her hand in marriage to anyone who could make her laugh.

"He who makes my daughter laugh shall marry her and be my heir," the king declared.

As soon as the princess saw Peter's ridiculous procession, she began to laugh as if she would never stop. But the king did not like the look of Peter.

"You can marry my daughter only if you can find a man who can drink every barrel in my castle," he said.

"Where will I find a man like that?" thought Peter.

Then he remembered the little old man in the forest. Maybe he would know. So off Peter went to find him.

Finally, Peter found the spot where he had chopped down the tree. The little old man was nowhere to be found. Instead, a man with a very sad face was sitting on the tree stump.

"Oh!" he cried, "I am so thirsty! No matter how much I drink, I cannot quench my thirst," sobbed the man. "What am I going to do?"

"Come with me," smiled Peter. "I think I have the answer."

He took the man back to the king's castle. There, the man drank every last barrel the king gave him.

"Can I marry your daughter now?" asked Peter.

But the king was still not satisfied.

"Not until you find a man who can eat a mountain of bread," he told Peter.

Peter thought for a while, then set out for the forest again to find the old man. There, he found a man holding his belly.

"Oh!" he cried, "I am so hungry!" No matter how much I eat, I cannot fill my belly," groaned the man. "What am I going to do?"

Peter led the man back to the castle. When they arrived, the king ordered a mountain of bread to be baked, as high as a castle. The hungry man gobbled every last crumb!

"Now can I marry your daughter?" asked Peter.

The king shook his head.

"First, you must bring me a ship that can sail on sea and land," he announced, certain the young man would fail.

By now, Peter knew exactly what to do. He went straight back to the forest. This time, the little old man was waiting for him.

The little old man listened carefully as Peter explained what he was looking for. Then he spoke.

"One good turn deserves another," he said. "Once, you gave me food and drink, so now I will give you the ship."

Imagine the king's surprise when Peter came sailing back across the fields.

"Is there anything this young man cannot do?" he cried. At last, the king realized he must allow Peter to marry his daughter.

The wedding took place right away, and the young couple were very happy together.

Many years later, when the old king finally died, Peter became king himself — a very happy ending for a young man people once made fun of!

The Three Billy Goats Gruff

Once upon a time, in a field far away, there lived three billy goat brothers. There was a big billy goat, with a great big belly and great big horns. There was a middle-size billy goat, with a middle-size belly and middle-size horns. And there was a little billy goat, with a teeny little belly and teeny little horns.

All three were brave and all had deep, gruff voices. Naturally, they called themselves the Billy Goats Gruff.

The three Billy Goats Gruff lived on a hill beside a bubbling river. Across the river was a meadow full of sweet, juicy clover – the goats' favourite food. The goats longed to visit the meadow, but to get there they had to cross a small rickety wooden bridge.

The Billy Goats Gruff would have happily crossed the small rickety bridge if it hadn't been for one thing – the meanest, fiercest troll you could possibly imagine lived beneath it. His eyes burned like fire and his warts bristled with thick, dark hairs. He had slimy fangs for teeth and claws as sharp as razor blades. He was always, always hungry and his favourite food was…GOAT!

Few dared cross that bridge and those that did were never heard of ever again. The Billy Goats Gruff were brave goats, but not stupid, so they stayed away from the bridge and ate the grass in their field. They ate and ate and ate, until one day there was nothing left but dirt.

As the goats looked across the river to the sweet, juicy clover on the other side, their bellies rumbled. Eventually, when they could bear it no more, they decided that they had no other choice but to cross the bridge.

"I'm not scared of that ugly troll," said the little Billy Goat Gruff. So he decided to go first.

The little Billy Goat Gruff's hooves clip-clopped over the bridge. He hadn't gone far when there was a terrifying **ROOOAAARRRR** and the ugly troll leaped out in front of him.

"Who's that clip-clopping over my bridge?" roared the troll.

"Only me, the teeny, littlest Billy Goat Gruff," replied the smallest billy goat bravely. "I'm on my way to the meadow to eat some sweet, juicy clover."

"Oh no, you're not," bellowed the troll. "I'm hungry and I'm going to gobble you up."

"Please don't do that," replied the brave little Billy Goat Gruff. "I'm just small and bony. My brother will be coming this way soon. He is far bigger and juicier than me. And he'll make a much better meal. I'm not worth wasting your time on."

The troll scratched a hairy wart and licked his rubbery lips hungrily. He hadn't eaten in a few days but decided he could wait just a little longer if it meant his next meal was even bigger.

"You do look a bit scrawny," he said slowly to the little billy goat. "Perhaps I could wait just a little longer for a bigger meal. Now SHOO before I change my mind."

So the little Billy Goat Gruff skipped across the bridge and was soon munching on the sweet, juicy clover on the other side.

Not long afterward, the middle-size Billy Goat Gruff began clip-clopping his way across the bridge.

"Who's that clip-clopping over my bridge?" snarled the troll nastily.

"Only me, the middle-sized Billy Goat Gruff," replied the next billy goat. "I'm on my way to the meadow to eat some sweet, juicy clover."

"Oh no, you're not," snarled the troll. "I'm going to gobble you up. I haven't eaten for a week and I'm starving," he bellowed. The troll opened his mouth wide and got ready to pounce.

"Why bother with me?" laughed the middle-sized billy goat. "I've hardly got any fat on me at all. Look, I'm all hair. If you wait a little longer, my big brother will be crossing your bridge. He's got a great, big belly and will fill you up in no time at all."

The troll looked at the middle-sized goat and rubbed his huge, round belly greedily. Maybe it wasn't so bad to wait just a bit longer for an even bigger meal.

"Okay," he said finally, "I'll wait for the biggest billy goat." And he let the middle-sized billy goat go.

The hungry troll waited for what seemed like a very long time. Then the bridge groaned and he heard a loud clip-clopping sound. The big Billy Goat Gruff was on his way.

"Who's that clip-clopping across my bridge?" roared the troll.

"Just me, the biggest Billy Goat Gruff of all," cried the last billy goat.

"Well, about time," shouted the angry troll. "I'm hungry. I've heard all about your great, big belly and can't wait to gobble you up."

"But you haven't heard about my great, big horns," roared the biggest Billy Goat Gruff crossly. He lowered his horns, scraped his hoof, and charged at the troll.

The terrified troll tried to run away but it was no good. SMACK – the biggest Billy Goat Gruff butted into him and tossed him high into the air. The troll somersaulted twice over the bridge, then – SPLASH – crashed into the water and disappeared.

The biggest Billy Goat Gruff didn't stop. He clip-clopped across the bridge to join the other two billy goats on the other side.

And so now the three Billy Goats Gruff live in the meadow full of sweet, juicy clover. Sometimes they visit their old field on the other side of the river because they can cross the bridge whenever they like. And as for the silly troll? Well, he was never seen again.

Alice and the White Rabbit

One day, Alice was sitting beside a river with her sister, when something curious happened. A white rabbit with pink eyes ran past.

"Oh, dear! Oh, dear! I shall be too late," he said. Then he took a watch out of his vest pocket and hurried on.

Alice quickly leaped to her feet and followed the rabbit down a large rabbit hole. The rabbit hole went straight on like a tunnel for some way, and then dipped so suddenly that Alice didn't have time to stop herself. She found herself falling down, down, down.

"I must be getting near the centre of the earth," Alice thought to herself.

Down, down, down, Alice kept falling. Suddenly she landed in a heap at the bottom. When she got up to look around she found herself in a long hall, lined with doors. At the end was a little three-legged glass table. There was nothing on it but a tiny golden key.

Alice tried the key in all the doors, but it wouldn't open any of them. Then she noticed a low curtain she had not seen before. Behind it was a tiny door.

She turned the key in the lock and it opened. The door led into a beautiful garden, but Alice could not even get her head through the doorway. She went back to the table and saw a little bottle labelled "DRINK ME!"

Once she was sure it wasn't poison, Alice drank it and shrank. But when she went back to the little door, she remembered that she had left the key on the table.

Alice didn't know what to do. Then she saw a cake marked "EAT ME!" She ate it and began to grow and grow. Soon she was so large her head touched the ceiling!

Alice sat down to cry. After a short while, a large pool surrounded her. Alice was wondering what to do, when who should come along but the white rabbit. He was carrying a pair of white gloves and a large fan.

"If you please, sir…" began Alice.

The rabbit dropped the gloves and fan, and scurried away.

"How strange everything is today," said Alice, picking up the gloves and the fan. "I'm not myself at all." Then she began fanning herself as she wondered who she might be instead.

After Alice had been fanning herself for some time, she looked down at her hands.

She was most surprised to see that she had put on one of the rabbit's little white gloves.

"I must be growing smaller again," she thought. Soon she realized that it was the fan that was making her grow smaller. She dropped it quickly before she shrank to nothing.

Alice ran to the door before she remembered that the key was still on the table. "Drat," said Alice. "Things can't possibly get any worse." But she was wrong. Her foot slipped and – SPLASH – she fell into her sea of tears.

"I wish I hadn't cried so much!" wailed Alice. Just then, she heard something splashing. It was a mouse.

"Oh Mouse, do you know the way out of this pool?" she asked. The Mouse didn't reply.

"Perhaps he speaks French," thought Alice. So she began again. "Où est mon chat?" which was the first sentence in her French book and meant "Where is my cat?"

The Mouse leaped out of the water in fright.

"Oh, I beg your pardon!" cried Alice quickly, afraid that she had hurt the Mouse's feelings. "I forgot mice don't like cats."

"Would you like cats if you were a mouse?" cried the Mouse.

"Perhaps not," replied Alice. "I promise I won't talk about cats again. Do you like dogs?"

The Mouse simply swam away.

"Do come back," cried Alice. "I won't talk about cats or dogs."

When the Mouse heard this, he swam back. "Let's go ashore and I'll tell you why I hate cats and dogs," he said.

By this time the pool was crowded with birds and animals. There was a duck and a dodo, a parrot and an eaglet, and several other curious creatures. Together they all swam to the shore.

The birds and animals were dripping wet. The first question, of course, was how to get everyone dry.

"The best thing to get us dry would be a caucus race," said the dodo.

"What is a caucus race?" asked Alice.

"You'll see," said the dodo, as he began to mark out the course. All the party were dotted along the course. Then they all began starting and stopping whenever they felt like it. It was impossible to tell when the race was over. However, after half an hour, they were all very dry.

"But who won?" asked the mouse.

"Everyone won," replied the dodo. "And Alice will give out the prizes."

Luckily, Alice had some candy in her pocket and handed them around.

"But she must have a prize," said the mouse.

"What else have you got in your pocket?" asked the dodo.

Alice handed over a thimble, and he gave it back to her saying, "I beg you to accept this thimble."

Alice accepted as solemnly as she could, and then they all sat down to hear mouse's tale. But so much had happened to Alice that she just couldn't concentrate and the mouse stomped away in a huff.

"I wish my cat, Dinah, were here," said Alice. "She'd soon fetch it back." Then she tried to tell her new friends about her cat. But she scared all the birds and little animals. They ran away, and poor Alice was alone once more.

The Ugly Duckling

It was a beautiful summer's day and the sun shone over the meadow. Down among the long grasses, near the edge of the brook, a mother duck quacked happily to herself. She was sitting patiently on her nest, waiting for her eggs to hatch.

She waited and waited, and then – CRACK, CRACK, CRACK, CRACK – one by one they started to hatch. Soon the mother duck was surrounded by a brood of beautiful, fluffy ducklings.

"Peep, peep!" they quacked. They were very pleased to see their mother at last.

Mother Duck stood up to check that they all had the right number of wings and webbed feet, and then quacked in dismay. The biggest egg still hadn't hatched. Mother Duck settled back on the nest and waited patiently. She waited and waited but nothing happened. Then she waited a bit more and still nothing happened.

"I'd leave it if I were you," said a passing duck. "Those big ones rarely hatch. You're wasting your time."

But the mother duck refused to listen. She sat on her nest and waited and waited. She waited for a very long time. Then, finally, there was an enormous CRACK, and out tumbled the biggest, ugliest duckling you can possibly imagine.

That afternoon, Mother Duck took her new family for a swimming lesson. "Quack, quack," she called, as she splashed into the water. "Follow me."

PLOP,
PLOP,
PLOP,
PLOP,
PLOP,

one by one the ducklings jumped in after her, even the big ugly duckling, who made quite a splash! Soon all of them were swimming beautifully. And the big, ugly duckling swam best of all.

The following morning, Mother Duck washed and groomed all her ducklings, and then took them to the farmyard.

"Don't stray from my side," she told the ducklings. "And whatever you do, please be polite to the big duck sitting on the island in the middle of the pond. She's the oldest and most important duck in the yard."

The farmyard was a very big and scary place. Hens scratched around in the dirt, a cat waited to pounce, and big ducks looked down their beaks as the ducklings waddled by.

"My, what beautiful ducklings," said the old duck kindly. "All except that big, ugly one," laughed another duck. All the other ducks turned and stared at the ugly duckling. Soon they were all laughing at him, even the oldest, most important duck.

Mother Duck and her ducklings settled down to their new life in the farmyard. All of them were very happy, except for the ugly duckling. He was sad because all the other farmyard animals laughed whenever they saw him. So one day, the ugly duckling decided to run away from the farmyard.

He didn't stop until he reached a marsh where wild ducks lived. But when the wild ducks saw him, they laughed and laughed, so the ugly duckling ran on.

He ran over fields and meadows, until he reached a rickety old house. The door had a hole in it, so the ugly duckling slipped in.

An old woman lived inside the house with her cat and her hen. She didn't have much but she was happy because the cat purred so nicely and the hen laid her eggs.

"Oh, goody," cried the old woman, when she saw the duckling. "Now I shall have duck eggs."

But, of course, the ugly duckling didn't lay any eggs, so the hen and the cat chased him away. The ugly duckling returned to the marsh, where he was alone once more.

Autumn arrived and the leaves fell from the trees. Then winter came and a cold wind blew snowflakes across the marsh. One evening, a flock of beautiful white birds with long graceful necks flew over the marsh. They were swans. "I wish I could fly with them," whispered the ugly duckling.

The winter grew colder and colder. The ugly duckling had to swim in circles to stop the water from freezing over. Then, one night, he fell asleep, and when he awoke he was stuck fast in the ice. Luckily for him, a passing farmer rescued him and took him home to his warm house.

When the ugly duckling had warmed up and was feeling better the farmer's children tried to play with him. But the ugly duckling was so scared by their excited shrieks that he flapped away in terror.

In his rush, he knocked over a churn of milk. The angry farmer's wife clapped her hands and he flapped into a sack of flour. The farmer's wife screamed. The children laughed and tried to catch him. The terrified duckling could take no more, and fled.

The poor, sad duckling returned to the frozen marsh. And there he remained throughout the long, harsh winter. Then, one morning, he awoke to a warm golden sun. As he stretched out to warm his feathers, he heard the sweet call of a cuckoo. Spring had arrived.

The ugly duckling spread out his wings and flew high into the air. He flew to a large garden, where willow trees dipped their long branches into a smooth pond. On the pond swam three beautiful white birds with long, graceful necks. It was the swans he had first seen so long ago.

The ugly duckling was so lonely that he decided to go and say hello. "They will send me away for being so ugly but I don't care," he said to himself. And so he landed by the pond and bent his head as he waited for the swans to chase him away.

But when he saw his reflection in the smooth water he gasped out loud. For, you see, he was no longer an ugly grey duckling. Instead, he was a beautiful white swan.

"Come, join us," called the youngest swan.

"Yes, please do," added the others. And they all swam around the ugly duckling, admiring his feathers and graceful arched neck.

"You really are the most beautiful swan of all," decided the oldest swan.

The ugly duckling ruffled his feathers with joy. Finally, he felt he belonged and was happy at last.

The Tortoise and the Hare

Once upon a time, there was a hare who was always boasting about how fast he was.

"I," he would say, puffing out his chest and flexing his legs, "am the speediest animal in the forest. I have never been beaten. I challenge anyone to try and beat me." And, of course, nobody took up the challenge because he was right – he was the fastest animal in the forest.

The animals who lived in the forest were becoming tired of Hare's bragging, until one day, much to everyone's surprise, after Hare had been boasting even more than normal, Tortoise replied:

"Okay, Hare. I'll race you."

"Whaaaaat?" laughed Hare. "You've got to be joking. Tortoise, you're the slowest animal in the forest. I'll run circles around you."

"You might be fast," replied Tortoise, "but speed isn't everything. Why don't we have a race? You can keep your boasting until you actually beat me."

"Speed might not be everything but it sure helps in a race," laughed Hare. He laughed so much that he fell to his knees and thumped the floor with his fist. He'd never heard of anything so ridiculous in his life.

That night, while the forest animals prepared the course, Tortoise went to bed early so he'd have a lot of energy for the race. Hare, meanwhile, stayed up late boxing with his friends. He knew he could beat the slow tortoise even if he was tired.

There was a buzz of excitement in the forest the next morning. No one had heard of Hare ever losing a race so this was going to be quite an event to watch! Everyone gathered at the starting line to watch the race begin. All the forest animals wanted Tortoise to win, but deep down they knew that Hare was the fastest.

Tortoise was already at the starting line, trying his best to look confident. He looked around for Hare, who had just arrived and was making his way to the starting line. He strutted toward Tortoise with his chest puffed out proudly. The crowd fell silent…

"On your marks, get set…GO!" cried the starting fox. And Hare flew off at high speed, leaving a cloud of smoke where he had just stood. The tortoise trudged behind much, much, much more slooooooowly.

Hare decided to take a quick look behind to see where the slow tortoise was. When he saw that Tortoise was far, far away, he decided to stop for breakfast. He feasted on some juicy carrots. Then he lay on his back, fiddled with his ears, and yawned.

"This is just too easy," he said, loud enough for just about all the animals in the forest to hear. "I think I'll have forty winks and catch up with him later." Soon he was snoring happily away. ZZZZZZZZZ!

Tortoise got to where Hare was lying, fast asleep. "Maybe I should wake him?" he thought, as he plodded past Hare. "No, I'm sure Hare wouldn't like that. He will wake up soon enough and come whizzing by."

And so Tortoise plodded on and on and on. Hare slept, on and on and on. In Hare's dreams, all the forest animals cheered and clapped as he streamed past the finish line.

The sun began to sink, and still Tortoise plodded on, and still Hare slept. The sun was just about to set when Hare awoke with a jolt. He could just see Tortoise in the distance, plodding slowly and carefully toward the finish line.

"Noooooooo!" cried Hare. He jumped to his feet and charged toward the finish as fast as he could. But he was too late. Tortoise was over the line before him. Hare had been beaten.
All the forest animals were there to cheer Tortoise.

After that, whenever anyone heard Hare boasting about his speed they reminded him about the day Tortoise beat him.
"Slow and steady won the race," they would say.

And all Hare could do was smile because, after all, they were without a doubt right.

Mowgli's Brothers

As the sun set over the jungle, the Wolf family stirred in their cave. Father Wolf prepared to go hunting, while Mother Wolf watched over her four playful cubs. All seemed well with the world, until suddenly – ROAR – a terrifying sound came from the jungle beyond.

Mother Wolf pulled her cubs close and shivered. It was Shere Khan the tiger, the most feared animal in the whole of the jungle. He was a cowardly beast, who killed without mercy. He was tracking something through the jungle, and he was getting closer.

Suddenly, the bushes rustled and Father Wolf prepared to pounce. But he just managed to stop himself when he saw that it wasn't the lion but a naked brown baby.

"A man cub!" gasped Father Wolf.

"I have never seen one. Bring it to me," said Mother Wolf.

Father Wolf gently picked up the baby in his jaws and dropped him among his own cubs. His sharp teeth didn't leave a mark on the baby's soft skin. The baby snuggled up against the Mother Wolf and smiled. Then the cave went black, as Shere Khan shoved his great head through the entrance.

"What do you want, Shere Khan?" asked Father Wolf.

"Give me the man cub," Shere Khan roared. "I've hunted him through the forest and he's mine."

Father Wolf knew that Shere Khan was too big to push his way into the cave, so he stood his ground.

"We wolves are a free people and take orders from no one. The man cub is ours," he replied.

Shere Khan howled with rage and Mother Wolf sprang to her feet.

"He shall not be killed. We will bring him up with our cubs. He will live to run with us and hunt with us. Now go!" she cried.

Shere Khan shook with fear. He might have challenged Father Wolf but never Mother Wolf. He backed out of the cave mouth and roared.

"We will see what the Pack Council has to say about you adopting a man cub," he growled, before disappearing into the jungle night.

Mother Wolf lay down beside her cubs and the little brown baby. The baby moved closer and gurgled.

"We will keep him," she declared. "And we'll call him Mowgli."

A month passed and a full moon rose over the jungle. The night of the Pack Council had arrived. Mother and Father Wolf took Mowgli and their cubs along to be inspected by the other wolves. Tonight they would decide if Mowgli could stay.

Akela, the leader of the pack, lay on a rock high above the others. Below him 40 or more wolves sat in a large circle. In the centre of the circle sat the playful cubs. One by one the wolves came forward to inspect the cubs until, at last, it was Mowgli's turn. Akela barely raised his head as he looked at Mowgli playing with some pebbles.

Then, suddenly, there was a roar from behind the rocks. It was Shere Khan. He dared not show his face but he had come to claim his prize.

"He's mine," he snarled. "Give him to me. You don't want a man cub in your pack."

Akela barely blinked an eye. "Ignore him," he cried. "He's no right to speak."

But some of the younger cubs agreed with Shere Khan. "He's right, we don't want a man cub in our pack," growled one.

"Silence," howled Akela. "You all know the rules. If two people, other than his parents, can come forward and speak in favour of him, he can stay. Who speaks for this cub?"

There was a noisy grunt and Baloo, the sleepy brown bear whose job it was to teach the wolf cubs the Law of the Jungle, lumbered into the circle.

"I speak for the man cub," he said. "He's harmless. Let him run with the pack. I myself will watch out for him."

"Good," said Akela. "But we need someone else."

Then a black shadow dropped down into the circle. It was Bagheera, the black panther. Everybody knew Bagheera and all respected him.

"The man cub is okay," he said in a voice as soft as wild honey dripping from a tree. "If you promise not to kill him, I'll give you a fat bull I've just killed."

The wolves licked their lips greedily, for they were always hungry. They talked noisily among themselves before quickly agreeing that Mowgli was welcome to stay for the price of a bull and Baloo's good word.

"So it is decided," said Akela. "He shall be allowed to run with the pack. He may be a help one day."

Many years passed and Mowgli and the wolf clubs grew big and strong. Mowgli learned all about the jungle. When he wasn't hunting and learning, he sat in the sun and slept and ate, then slept again. When he was dirty or hot he swam in the forest pools. What Father Wolf didn't teach him, he learned from his friends Baloo and Bagheera.

Some nights Mowgli would creep down to the village and watch people in their huts, but he didn't trust men because he knew they set traps in the jungle. Every now and then, Mowgli would bump into Shere Khan. The cowardly tiger had grown braver as Akela grew older, and now he was friendly with some of the younger wolves. Bagheera warned Mowgli that Shere Khan would try to kill him one day. Mowgli would simply laugh.

"But I have the Pack and you and Baloo to protect me.
He wouldn't dare," he'd say.

Bagheera tried to explain that Akela was old and weak and
wouldn't be the Pack leader for much longer. Once he was gone,
the other wolves might not be so keen to protect a man cub. But
Mowgli was young and would not listen. After all, he had pulled
thorns from the wolves' paws and hunted alongside them. They
wouldn't let a tiger kill him.

But the wise old panther was right. Before long, Akela was so feeble that another wolf decided to take over the Pack. And when he did, the wolves held a Pack Council and called for Mowgli's blood.

"Quick," Bagheera hissed to Mowgli.
"Go down to the village and fetch the Red Flower."
"Red Flower?" asked Mowgli.
By Red Flower, Bagheera meant fire, only jungle creatures don't like to call it by its proper name.

"You know how scared all the animals are of man's fire," said Bagheera. "Now go!"

Mowgli raced down to the village and dipped a dry branch into a fire, then ran to the Council. Akela lay beside his rock, weak but ready to fight, while Shere Khan spoke.

"Give me the boy," he roared.

"He is one of us," replied Akela weakly.

"And I paid for him with a bull," added Bagheera.

"What do we care about that," snarled the Pack.

"If you let him go, I will not fight you. That will save at least three lives."

But the snarling, snapping Pack would not listen. They could smell blood.

Mowgli jumped to his feet and waved his burning branch at the Pack. They cowered in fear.

"If you let Akela go, I will go to the village and live among people," cried Mowgli. "But before I go, I must do one thing." He grabbed Shere Khan by the scruff of his neck and beat him around the head with the burning branch. The cowardly tiger whimpered and whined.

"Now go," he cried. "But remember this – next time I see you, I will kill you."

Then he whirled the burning branch around his head until the cowardly tiger and treacherous wolves scampered away in fright.

With tears in his eyes, Mowgli went to say farewell to Mother and Father Wolf and the four cubs.

"Don't forget us," said the cubs. "When you are a man, come and visit."

"Come soon," said Father Wolf.

"Come soon," said Mother Wolf. "We will miss you."

"Don't worry. I'll be back soon," said Mowgli, before setting off to his new life among men.

Goldilocks and the Three Bears

Once there was a beautiful little girl called Goldilocks, with golden hair that gleamed in the sunshine. But although she looked like an angel, Goldilocks didn't behave like one. She was often naughty, and didn't do as she was told.

One day, Goldilocks went out to play in the meadow.

"Stay close to home," her mother reminded her. "Don't go into the forest, or you will get lost."

At first, Goldilocks did as she was told. But then she started to get bored.

"Why shouldn't I go into the forest if I want to?" she muttered to herself. "I won't get lost if I stay on the path."

When her mother wasn't looking, Goldilocks skipped across the meadow and into the forest. She had so much fun kicking leaves and climbing trees, she forgot all about staying on the path. It wasn't until her tummy began to rumble that she saw she was lost.

"Drat!" she said. "I'm hungry!"

Suddenly, Goldilocks sniffed a whiff of something yummy, floating on the breeze.

"Hhhmmm!" she said, following her nose. "That smells delicious."

The smell led Goldilocks to the door of a small house in the trees. She knocked loudly on the door. RAT-A-TAT-TAT! There was no reply.

"I can't see anyone," said Goldilocks, peeping through the window. "They must be out." Then she opened the door and marched right in.

On the kitchen table were three bowls of sticky, syrupy porridge: a great big one, a middle-size one, and a teeny-weeny one.

In an instant, Goldilocks dipped a spoon into the biggest bowl and slurped the porridge hungrily.

"OUCH!" she spluttered. "That's too hot!"

Next she tried the middle-size bowl of porridge. YUCK! It was far too cold. So Goldilocks dipped her spoon into the teeny-weeny bowl and tasted it. YUM! It was just right. She gobbled it all up quickly!

When she had finished licking the syrupy spoon, Goldilocks looked around the room. There were three comfortable chairs by the fire: a great big one, a middle-size one, and a teeny-weeny one.

"Just the place for a nap," yawned Goldilocks. She flopped down onto the biggest chair.

"OUCH!" she complained, jumping up. "That's too hard!"

The middle-size chair was even worse. It was far too soft and squishy.

So Goldilocks tried the teeny-weeny chair. It was very small, but finally she managed to squeeze herself onto the seat. Suddenly, there was a loud SNAP! then CRASH! Goldilocks fell to the floor in a heap of broken chair legs.

"Oh dear!" she cried, jumping up. "Maybe no one will notice."

Then Goldilocks saw a staircase in the corner of the room. At the top, she found a room with three beds in it: a great big one, a middle-size one, and a teeny-weeny one.

"I'll just have a little lie down," Goldilocks decided. So she bounced onto the biggest bed. OOF!
It was far too lumpy.

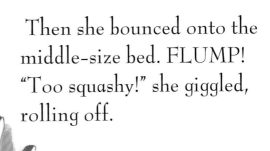

Then she bounced onto the middle-size bed. FLUMP!
"Too squashy!" she giggled, rolling off.

Goldilocks sat on the teeny-weeny bed and tried a little bounce. It was just right, so she lay down. Soon she was fast asleep. She didn't know the owners of the house were on their way home.

The owners of the house were a family of hungry bears: a big daddy bear, a middle-size mummy bear, and a teeny-weeny baby bear! As soon as they got home, the bear family went straight to the table to eat their breakfast. . .

"Who's been eating my porridge?" growled Daddy Bear, peering in his bowl.

"And who's been eating my porridge?" growled Mummy Bear.

"At least you've got some left!" cried Baby Bear. "Look! Mine's all gone. Even the spoon is licked clean!"

Daddy Bear looked around the room.

"Who's been sitting in my chair?" he growled, examining the cushion.

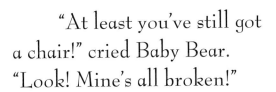

Who's been sitting in my chair?" growled Mummy Bear.

"At least you've still got a chair!" cried Baby Bear. "Look! Mine's all broken!"

The three bears went upstairs.

"Who's been lying on my bed?" growled Daddy Bear, examining the pillow.

"And who's been lying on my bed?" growled Mummy Bear.

"At least there's no one in your bed!" cried Baby Bear. "Look who's in mine!"

At that very moment, Goldilocks woke up with a start and saw the three bears.

At first, she thought she was dreaming. But when the biggest bear growled, "WHO ARE YOU?" she knew it wasn't a dream. Goldilocks leaped out of bed, ran down the stairs, and out of the door. She did not stop running until she had reached her own home.

And from that day on, Goldilocks changed her ways. Not only did she look like an angel, but she tried to behave like one, too.

Well...for most of the time, anyway!

The Six Swans

Once, in a faraway land, a king was hunting in the forest when it began to get dark. The king looked around and saw that he was lost. Suddenly, he spotted an old woman.

"My dear lady," he cried. "Can you show me the way back to the palace?"

"Yes, your majesty," answered the old woman, who was really a witch. "But only if you promise to do something for me."

"What is it?" asked the king.

"I have a beautiful daughter," replied the witch. "If you promise to marry her, I will show you the way. If not, I will leave you alone in the dark with the hungry wild animals."

The king was so frightened that he promised to marry the girl. The witch led him to her cottage, where her daughter was waiting.

It was true what the old woman had said.
Her daughter was beautiful, but there was
something about her that made the king shudder.
However, he'd given his word, so he lifted
her onto his horse. Then the witch
showed him the way home.

The king married the girl the very next day.
The king had been married before and had six sons
and a daughter whom he loved more than anything in
the world. But he did not tell the queen about them
because he did not think she would be kind to them.

The king decided to hide his children in a castle,
deep in a forest. Even the king himself didn't
know the way there. He had to roll a ball of magic
string through the forest to show him the path.

The king secretly visited his children every evening. But the new queen soon began to wonder where the king went in the forest every night and what he did. Whenever she tried to follow him she would get lost and have to return to the palace.

The queen tricked one of the king's servants into telling her the secret. When the queen found out about the king's children she knew she had to find them.

The next day the queen searched the castle until she found the ball of magic string. Then, using a spell she had learned from her mother, she made some magic shirts of white silk.

When the king went hunting the next day, she took the ball of magic string and the shirts, and went into the forest.

The six sons thought it was their father coming toward the castle and rushed out to hug him. As soon as the queen saw the boys, she threw the magic shirts over their heads. In an instant, they turned into white swans and flew away.

In the evening, when the king went to visit his children, he found no one but his daughter.

"My brothers flew away," she told her father sadly. The king was heartbroken.

"You must come home with me, where it is safe," he told her. But the girl didn't want to leave in case her brothers returned. She begged to stay in the castle one more night. Finally, the king agreed. When no swans returned to the castle, the princess decided to go and look for her brothers. She searched all night, until at last she found a hunter's hut. Inside were six little beds, so she hid under one and closed her eyes.

Suddenly, there was the sound of beating wings. Six white swans flew in through the window and landed on the beds.

The girl watched in amazement as the
swans blew on one another. At once, their feathers
fell off, just like shirts.

"My brothers!" she cried.

The six boys were overjoyed to see their sister.
But they were also worried.

"You can't stay here," they said. "It's a robbers' den.
If they find you, they will be angry. Each day, we are human
for only fifteen minutes before we turn into swans again."

"How can I free you from the spell?"
asked their sister.

"It is too hard to ask you.
You must sew six shirts from tiny
starflower petals," said one brother.
"And you must not speak or laugh
for six years."

"I will do it," the sister replied.
And with that, her brothers turned
into swans again.

The princess set off to start
collecting starflowers. She sat
down by a tree and
began to sew.

Before long, a king from another land rode by with his men.

"What are you doing?" asked the king. Of course, the girl would not speak. She just carried on sewing.

The king's heart was touched. He wanted to protect this beautiful silent girl, so he took her home and showered her with gifts. Still the girl did not speak. She just carried on sewing. But the king soon fell in love with her and they married.

The king's mother was jealous of the new queen and wanted to get rid of her. When the girl had her first baby, the king's mother stole the child and gave it to a woodcutter. She told everyone the queen had given away the baby. Of course, the queen would not speak to say it was a lie. She just bit her lip and carried on sewing.

Luckily, the king did not believe his mother.

"My wife is too good to do a wicked thing like that!" he said.

A year later, the queen had another baby. The king's mother did the same thing. She stole the child and gave it to the woodcutter.

"Now do you believe me?" she demanded.

The king shook his head.

"If she could speak, she would tell us she is innocent," he cried.

But when their third child disappeared, the king started to have doubts.

"All my wife wants to do is sew all day," he thought. "Maybe my mother is telling the truth."

The king begged his wife to defend herself, but she would not speak.

Sadly, the king decided she must be guilty.

"You will be punished in the morning," he told her.

The queen sewed all night. It was the last night of the six years she had been given to make the starflower shirts and she had not once uttered a word or laughed.

At sunrise, the six shirts were almost finished. Only one sleeve was missing from the last shirt.

As the king's men took the queen to see the king, the air was filled with the sound of beating wings. Six white swans landed.

The queen threw the starflower shirts over their heads. At once, their feathers vanished. Her six brothers stood before her, though the youngest still had the wing of a swan instead of an arm.

"At last I can speak," she sobbed. Then she kissed her husband and told him what had happened and how the king's mother had taken their children to the woodcutter.

When the king heard the truth, he banished his mother forever. The king had the woodcutter bring him his children who were all happy to see their parents.

"Your six brothers must come and live with us, too," cried the king to his wife. "Then our whole family can live together in happiness."

And that is exactly what happened.

Rikki-Tikki-Tavi

Rikki-Tikki-Tavi was a small furry mongoose. He looked like a little cat in his fur and his tail, but his head and the way he acted were more like a weasel. He had shining pink eyes and a twitching pink nose. He could fluff up his tail until it looked like a bottle brush, and his war cry, as he scuttled through the long grass, was "*Rikk-tikk-tikki-tikki-tchk!*"

Rikki-Tikki lived a happy life with his parents in the jungle. Then one day, a great summer flood washed him from his burrow. It swept him on and on, and carried him, kicking and clucking, down a roadside ditch. He found a little wisp of grass, and clung to it until he lost his senses. When he revived, he was lying in the hot sun on the middle of a path in front of a house. A young boy was saying:

"Look, Mum! A dead mongoose."

"No, he's not dead," replied the boy's mother. "Let's take him in to dry. The poor little thing is exhausted."

The little boy was called Teddy and he lived in the bungalow with his parents. The family were so kind that Rikki-Tikki decided to stay.

The first night, he slept on Teddy's pillow. And the following morning he ate breakfast and took it in turns to sit on all their laps, because every well-brought-up mongoose always hopes to be a house mongoose some day.

Then Rikki-Tikki decided to explore the yard. He hadn't got far when he heard somebody crying. It was Darzee, the tailorbird and his wife.

"What's the matter?" asked Rikki-Tikki.

"Nag has eaten one of our babies," sobbed Darzee.

"Oh, dear," said Rikki-Tikki. "But who's Nag?"

Before Darzee could answer, there was a loud hiss and a hideous black cobra slithered into sight. He was five feet long from tongue to tail.

"I am Nag," hissed the beast. "Be afraid. Be very afraid."

For a moment Rikki-Tikki couldn't help feeling just the tiniest bit afraid because, as everyone knows, cobras have a deadly bite. But it is impossible for a mongoose to stay frightened for long. Although he had never met a cobra before, he knew that it was every brave mongoose's duty to fight deadly snakes. He held his tail high and puffed out his cheeks. He looked terrifying, and Nag began to shake.

Then Nag saw the grass rustle behind Rikki-Tikki and knew that help was at hand. He tried to distract him.

"Hey, let's talk," he hissed. "You eat eggs. Why should I not eat birds?"

"Watch out behind you!" cried Darzee.

Rikki-Tikki leaped up into the air and just missed being struck by Nagaina, Nag's wicked wife. Rikki-Tikki landed on her back and bit, before jumping clear of the wriggling beast.

Rikki-Tikki's eyes glowed red with rage as Nag and Nagaina disappeared into the grass. He didn't follow because he wasn't sure he could take on two snakes. But he was still proud that he had managed to escape a blow from behind.

Teddy came running down the path to pat Rikki-Tikki. But just as Teddy was stooping down, something moved in the dust.

"Be careful. I am death," a tiny voice hissed. It was Karait, the dusty brown snakeling. His bite is as dangerous as any cobra's, but because he is so small nobody fears him.

Karait lunged and Rikki-Tikki jumped on his head and bit. As Rikki-Tikki rolled away, Karait lay paralyzed.

"Quick!" Teddy called to his parents. "Our mongoose is killing a snake."

Teddy's mum and dad came running out. Teddy's mum picked up the mongoose and hugged him for saving Teddy's life.

Rikki-Tikki was about to eat up Karait, as is family custom, when he remembered that a full stomach makes a slow mongoose, and if he wanted all his strength to fight Nag and his wife, he needed to be alert.

That night, Teddy carried him off to bed and insisted Rikki-Tikki slept under his chin. But as soon as Teddy was asleep, Rikki-Tikki went exploring.

In the dark, he met Chuchundra, the musk-rat, who was creeping around by the wall.

"Please don't eat me," said Chuchundra, crying.

"I won't eat you," replied Rikki-Tikki. "But Nag is in the yard, so you must be careful."

"Shh! Nag is everywhere, Rikki-Tikki. Can't you *hear*?"

Rikki-Tikki listened. The house was quiet, but he thought he could hear the faintest *scratch-scratch* — the dry scratch of snake's scales on bricks. Rikki-Tikki went into the bathroom and heard Nag and Nagaina whispering outside in the moonlight.

"When all the people have gone," said Nagaina, "HE will have to leave, then the yard will be ours once more. Now, bite the big man first. Then we will hunt Rikki-Tikki together."

"So long as the house is empty, we are the king and queen of the yard; and remember that as soon as our eggs in the melon bed hatch, our children will need room and quiet. And no Rikki-Tikki!" Nagaina hissed.

Rikki-Tikki shook with rage at hearing this, but he hid as the giant cobra slithered into the bathroom. Then he watched as the loathsome creature coiled himself around the water jug lying in wait to bite Teddy's father.

Rikki-Tikki waited until Nag had fallen asleep, then he jumped. He sank his fangs into the cobra's head and held on tight as he thrashed around. Rikki-Tikki bit harder as he was whipped around the bathroom. He was sure he was going to be beaten to death. Then, suddenly, a gun went off and Nag was no more. Teddy's father had heard the noise and now he had shot the wicked snake.

"Look! The mongoose has saved OUR lives now," he shouted to his wife.

The following morning, Rikki-Tikki was feeling very pleased with himself but just a tiny bit afraid.

"Now I have Nagaina to settle with," Rikki-Tikki told himself. He rushed outside to find Darzee singing in his nest.

"Where is Nagaina?" enquired Rikki-Tikki.

"Nag is dead, Nag is dead," sang Darzee.

"Oh, do be quiet," snapped Rikki-Tikki. "Nag may be dead but Nagaina is still alive and kicking. Where is Nagaina?"

"For the great, the beautiful Rikki-Tikki's sake I will stop," said Darzee. "What is it, O Killer of the terrible Nag?"

"Where is Nagaina?" he asked for the third time.

"On the garbage pile beside the stable, mourning Nag," replied Darzee.

"Do you know where she keeps her eggs?" asked Rikki-Tikki.

"In the melon bed," replied Darzee slowly. "You're not going to eat them, are you?"

"Not exactly," replied the mongoose. "Now if you could just keep Nagaina busy, you'll soon see what I have in mind."

Now Darzee was a bit of a scatterbrain and thought that just because Nagaina's children were born in eggs like his own, they should be left well alone. But his wife was a sensible bird and knew that young cobras were born out of cobras' eggs. So she left Darzee to guard the nest and fluttered over to Nagaina.

"Oh, my poor wing is broken!" she cried. Then she fluttered helplessly near Nagaina.

"Well, you chose a rotten place to fly with a broken wing," hissed the wicked cobra, slithering across the dust after her. "Look at me!" Darzee's wife knew that if a bird looks at a snake's eyes it gets so frightened it cannot move, so she carried on fluttering by Nagaina.

As soon as the coast was clear, Rikki-Tikki rushed to the cobra's nest and began to smash the eggs. Now there would be no young cobras to terrorize everyone. He had just picked up the last egg when Darzee's wife started to scream.

"Quick, Rikki-Tikki!" she cried. "Nagaina is up at the house and is going to harm the family."

Rikki-Tikki leaped to his feet and scuttled to the house as fast as he could.

On the porch, Teddy and his mom were sitting as still as stone. Their faces were white. Nagaina was coiled up beside Teddy's chair. She was ready to strike.

"Stay still, Teddy. You musn't move," his mom told him.

"Turn and fight, Nagaina," cried Rikki-Tikki.

"All in good time," she said without taking her eyes off Teddy.

"Look at this egg," cried Rikki-Tikki, holding up the last remaining cobra egg. "This is the only one left. I've smashed all the others."

Nagaina whipped her head around and howled. And as she did, Teddy's dad pulled Teddy to safety.

"Give me the egg, Rikki-Tikki. If you give me the last of my eggs I will go away and never come back."

But Rikki-Tikki knew that she was lying. Nagaina struck out and Rikki-Tikki leaped out of the way. Again and again she struck and each time Rikki-Tikki danced out of the way. But the young mongoose had forgotten the egg.

Suddenly, Nagaina caught it in her mouth and flew like an arrow down the path. Rikki-Tikki raced after her. She went down into a rat hole where she had lived with Nag. Rikki-Tikki bit onto the end of her tail and followed her into the hole.

It was dark in the hole, and Rikki-Tikki didn't know when it might open out and give Nagaina room to attack. But he didn't let go of her tail.

Now, all animals know that it isn't a good idea to follow a cobra into its hole, and Darzee the bird knew this. He started to sing a sad song. "It is all over," cried Darzee sadly. He was making up a song about Rikki-Tikki's bravery, when the mongoose himself popped out of the hole, licking his whiskers.

"It's all over," he said proudly. "The cobras are dead."

Rikki-Tikki curled himself up in the grass and slept until late in the afternoon, for he had had a busy day.

When Rikki-Tikki woke he went to the house.

"He saved our lives!" said Teddy's mom happily.

And that's the last time a cobra ever dared set foot inside the walls of Rikki-Tikki's yard.

Puss in Boots

Once upon a time, there was a poor old miller who had three sons. When the miller died he left his mill to his eldest son. He left his donkey to his middle son. And he left his cat to his youngest son, who was called Jack. It was a very fine cat, with handsome silver whiskers and beautiful emerald eyes, but Jack was so poor that he could barely afford to feed himself, let alone the poor creature as well.

"What am I going to do with you?" Jack asked the cat. "My brothers will be able to make a living with their mill and donkey, while you and I will probably starve." He tickled the purring cat's soft belly and shook his head sadly.

Well, Jack might have spoken to the cat, but he certainly didn't expect it to answer him, so you can imagine his surprise when the cat said:

"Don't worry about a thing. Just give me a pair of boots, a hat, and a sack and you'll soon discover that I'm worth much more than a silly old mill or a stupid donkey."

Jack quickly saw that this was
no ordinary puss, so he took his last
coins and bought a hat and a pair
of fine boots. Then he went to his
brother's mill to fetch a sack.

Jack presented both to the
cat, who was delighted. He pulled
on the boots and strutted up
and down in front of his master.
The cat looked so funny that Jack
laughed and laughed until his sides
hurt. There and then, he decided
to call him Puss in Boots.

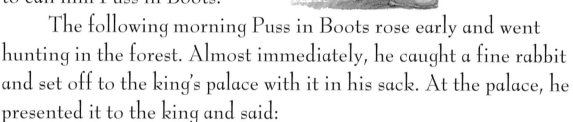

The following morning Puss in Boots rose early and went
hunting in the forest. Almost immediately, he caught a fine rabbit
and set off to the king's palace with it in his sack. At the palace, he
presented it to the king and said:

"This is a gift from my master, the Marquis of Carabas"
(a name that he had at that very moment conjured up in his head).

The king was delighted with the gift and very amused to see
a cat wearing such fine boots. He couldn't wait to see who owned
such a fine pet.

"Perhaps I could call on your master and thank him myself,"
he suggested.

Well, you might be surprised to learn that Puss in Boots quickly gave the king directions to his master's castle. The king promised he would call the next day, and bring his beautiful daughter, Melissa, with him.

The next morning, Puss in Boots took Jack to a lake on the very road that he had told the king his master's castle was on. The cunning puss told his master that if he bathed in the water, it would bring him good luck. As soon as Jack dived into the water, Puss in Boots hid his clothes and ran to meet the king.

"Help, help!" cried Puss, as soon as he spotted the king's carriage. "Robbers have stolen my master's clothes."

Without a moment's hesitation, the king told his servants to fetch the spare clothes he always carried in the back of his carriage and give them to Jack.

Jack got dressed in a suit of the finest cloth. He looked like such a fine gentleman that the king happily invited Jack to join him and Princess Melissa in the royal carriage. Jack looked so handsome that the princess blushed prettily and fell in love with him on the spot.

Once they were all safely in the carriage, Puss in Boots got down on all fours and raced ahead. He came to a field where some men were working.

"Good men," Puss began. "When the king comes passing by in his carriage you must tell him that the fields in which you work belong to the Marquis of Carabas. If you don't, it'll be off with your heads!"

Sure enough, when the king passed the field of workers he stopped and asked who owned the land.

"Why, the Marquis of Carabas, your Majesty," they all replied, for no one wanted to see if the cat's threats would come true.

The king was secretly impressed, even though poor Jack looked a little confused.

Puss in Boots, realizing his plan was working, did the same thing again. All the farmers and tradesmen the king met said:

"Everything around here belongs to the Marquis of Carabas."

The king looked at Jack sitting beside his blushing daughter and smiled. "He's so handsome and rich, he'd make a fine husband for my daughter," he thought to himself.

As it happened, the fields and lands really belonged to a fierce giant who lived in a castle at the end of the road. Puss in Boots hurried to the castle and knocked on the door.

"WHO GOES THERE?" roared the big, fierce giant.

"Just me," replied Puss in Boots. "I've travelled from far away because I've heard that you are a wonderful magician. I have heard that you can change yourself into any animal you want."

"True," said the giant, who was very vain and a bit of a show-off. Then he turned himself into a huge lion.

"That's very impressive," said Puss in Boots from where he was hiding behind a cupboard.

"But I bet a huge fellow like you couldn't turn yourself into something small, such as…a teeny-tiny mouse!"

"Easy-peasy," boasted the giant, immediately turning himself into a little brown mouse. In a flash, the cunning puss pounced on the mouse and gobbled him up.

Just then, the king's carriage arrived at the castle. Puss in Boots raced out to welcome him.

"Welcome to the Marquis of Carabas's humble home," said the cat, with a sweeping bow.

"You mean to say that this is all yours?" said the king, turning to Jack. At first Jack looked confused but when Puss in Boots winked at him, he decided to hold his tongue. He held out his hand and led Princess Melissa into the castle.

The king was so impressed that when Jack, or the Marquis of Carabas as he was now called, asked him for his daughter's hand in marriage, he quickly agreed. Indeed, he heartily congratulated himself on finding such a fine son-in-law. And from that day forth, the Marquis of Carabas, the princess, and, of course, Puss in Boots lived happily ever after.

Tales of Black Beauty

The first place I can remember was a large meadow with a pond. There were shady trees that leaned over it, and rushes and water-lilies grew at the deep end. On one side of the meadow was a plowed field, and on the other was our master's house.

I lived in the meadow with my mother and lived off her milk while I was very young. Then, when I was old enough to eat grass my mother went out to work during the day, and at night I would lie down close to her.

In the meadow were six young colts. They were all older than me. Some were nearly as big as grown-up horses. I had great fun with those colts, galloping around the field, as fast as we could go. Sometimes we played rough, biting and kicking. Then, one day, my mother took me aside.

"Those colts are very good colts but they are cart horses and bad mannered. You have been well bred. You have never seen me bite or kick. I hope you will grow up gentle and good. You must work hard, lift your feet up when you trot, and never bite or kick, even in play."

I have never forgotten those wise words. I knew my mother was a wise horse, and our master thought a great deal of her. Her name was Duchess, but he often called her Pet.

Our master was a good, kind man. We were always well fed and had clean stables. He spoke as kindly to us as he did to his own children. We were all very fond of him. All the horses would go to him, although I think we were his favourites.

Years passed and I grew handsome and strong. I had a bright black, shiny coat, one white foot, and a pretty white star on my forehead. My master did not want to sell me until I was four years old. He said colts shouldn't work like horses until they were properly grown up.

When the time came that I was four years old, Squire Gordon came to see me. He checked my eyes, my mouth, and my legs. Then I had to walk and trot and gallop in front of him. He said he would have me once I was ready to ride and drive in a carriage.

My master decided to break me in himself so I wouldn't get scared or hurt. We started the very next day. In case you don't know what breaking in is, I'll explain. It means teaching a horse to wear a saddle and bridle and to learn how to carry someone on its back.

At first it felt strange to have somebody on my back, but I felt proud to carry my master. Next, I was broken to harness. My master often drove me alongside my mother because she was calm and steady. She told me the better I behaved, the better I'd be treated. More good words.

Before long I was taken to Birtwick Park, where I would live with Squire Gordon. It was a large house that was surrounded by gardens. There was also an orchard and then the stables.

The stables were very roomy with a large swinging window that opened into the yard. I was put in a fine stall next to a little fat grey pony. His name was Merrylegs and he was ridden by the squire's children. He was a fine little pony and we quickly became great friends. There was also a chestnut mare in the stable, called Ginger. Ginger was bad tempered and snapped and bit.

The next day, James the stable boy fitted me with a bridle and got me ready for Squire Gordon to ride. I am pleased to say, my new master was a very good rider. When we got back from our first ride, his wife was waiting for him.

"Well, my dear," she said, "how do you like him?"

"He is perfect," replied Squire Gordon. "What shall we call him?"

"What about Ebony?" she said. "He is as black as ebony."

"No, not Ebony."

"What about Blackbird?"

"No, he is far too handsome for that."

"Yes," she agreed. "He really is a beauty. What about calling him Black Beauty?"

"Perfect," smiled Squire Gordon.

And so that was my new name.

Although I missed my mother and the meadow, I was quite happy in my new home. Sometimes I was taken out with Ginger. At first she laid back her ears and I was wary of her, but soon we became friends.

One day Ginger told me about her old life. No one had ever been kind to her. That was why she was so bad tempered.

But life was much better at Squire Gordon's, and little by little, she grew much more gentle and cheerful.

My life at Squire Gordon's was a good one. The coachman was called John Manly. He was a kind man, who talked to me a great deal and often took me out with the carriage. James, the stable boy, was just as gentle and friendly.

One day my master and mistress decided to visit friends two days' journey away. James was to drive them and Ginger and I were to pull the carriage. The first day's drive was long and tiring, so we were pleased to stop at a hotel for the night. The two grooms who worked there took care of us very well. They groomed us and bedded us down in clean stalls. Later, a young man smoking a pipe came in for a gossip. "Towler," said the groom. "Put down your pipe, then go up to the loft and put some hay in this horse's rack, please." Towler did as he was asked. Later James came in to check on us, and then the door was locked.

I awoke feeling very uncomfortable. The air was thick and choking. I heard Ginger coughing, and one of the other horses seemed restless. It was dark and I couldn't see anything, but the stable was full of smoke and I could hardly breathe.

The trapdoor to the loft had been left open and I could hear cracking and snapping. I did not know what it was but I trembled with fright.

At last I heard footsteps and one of the grooms burst in and began to untie the horses. But he was so scared that he frightened all of us horses and we refused to budge.

Then I heard a cry of "Fire!" and the other groom came in. He calmly got one horse out and went back for another. The next thing I heard was James's gentle voice.

"Come, Beauty, on with your bridle. We'll soon be out of this." Then he took the scarf off his neck, and tied it lightly over my eyes, and still speaking to me in a soft voice he led me out of the stable.

When we were safe in the yard, he slipped the scarf off and asked somebody to stay with me. Then he went back in. I whinnied loudly. Ginger told me later that my whinny gave her the courage to come out. It seemed forever before James and Ginger finally emerged from the flames. Then, at last, the firefighters arrived and the fire was put out.

The next day I heard that the fire was started by that young man's pipe. After that terrible night we couldn't wait to get back to Birtwick Park. One night, and not long afterward, I was awoken by a bell. John came racing in carrying my bridle and saddle.

"Wake up, Beauty," he called. "We must race through the night."

John tacked me up quickly and rode me up to the hall. The squire stood by the door with a lamp in his hand.

"Your mistress is very ill," he cried. "There's not a moment to lose. Give this note to Dr. White, then give Beauty a rest before riding back again."

We rode like the wind through the night and soon delivered the note to the good doctor. The doctor's horse had been out all day so although I had galloped all the way, I carried the doctor back to the Park as fast as I could.

After that night I was ill. I began to shake and tremble and shiver all over with cold. Even though I couldn't speak, John seemed to know how I felt. He covered me with rugs and nursed me night and day. My master also came to see me.

"My poor Beauty!" he said one day. "You saved your mistress's life!" I was very glad to hear that and, from what the doctor said, if we had been a little while longer, it would have been too late.

John told my master that he had never seen a horse go so fast in his life, as if I knew what the matter was. Of course I did, I thought. I knew that my mistress's life was in danger.

I do not know how long I was ill, but I eventually got better. When I recovered, I discovered that there were going to be great changes.

I had now lived at Birtwick Park for three years. We heard from time to time that our mistress was ill and the doctor was often at the house. Then we heard that our mistress had to go to a warm country to get better. The household and stables were to be broken up.

Merrylegs was given to the local priest. Joe was to go with him so I knew he'd be well looked after. And Ginger and I were sold to the Earl of Wicklow and went to live at Earlshall Park. And so the next chapter of my life began.

Chicken Licken

One day, Chicken Licken was scratching for food in the woods when, BOINK! an acorn from an oak tree fell onto her head.

"Ruffle my feathers!" said Chicken Licken. "The sky is falling down. I must tell the king at once." And off she ran as fast as her legs would carry her.

On her way, Chicken Licken met Cocky Locky.

"Where are you going, Cocky Locky?" she puffed.

"To the woods to scratch for bugs," replied Cocky Locky.

"Oh, don't go!" clucked Chicken Licken, in alarm. "I was there a moment ago, and the sky fell on my head! I'm off to tell the king right away."

"Goodness!" clucked Cocky Locky. "I'd better come with you." And off they hurried.

On their way, Chicken Licken and Cocky Locky met Ducky Lucky.

"Where are you going, Ducky Lucky?" asked Chicken Licken.

"To the pond for a swim," replied Ducky Lucky.

"Oh, stop, Ducky Lucky!" squawked Chicken Licken. "The sky in the woods is falling down! We're off to tell the king at once."

"Babbling brooks!" quacked Ducky Lucky. "Let's go. There's no time to lose."

They had just set off again, when Ducky Lucky saw Goosey Loosey.

"Oh, Goosey Loosey," he quacked. "Something terrible has happened. Chicken Licken said the sky in the woods is falling down. We have to tell the king right away!"

Goosey Loosey was very worried. "I'd better come, too," she honked.

So the four birds went along until they met Foxy Loxy.

"Good day to you all!" said the crafty fox. "Where are you going this fine day?"

Chicken Licken puffed up her chest importantly. "We're off to see the king," she announced. "The sky fell on my head in the woods. We must tell him at once. The king will know what to do."

Foxy Loxy grinned slyly. "But you are going the long way to the king's palace. Let me show you the quickest way there," he said, leading the way.

So Chicken Licken, Cocky Locky, Ducky Lucky, and Goosey Loosey all followed Foxy Loxy. So they went along until they came to a narrow, dark hole in the hillside.

"Follow me!" said sly Foxy Loxy. With that, he led Goosey Loosey, Ducky Lucky, and Cocky Locky into his den. Chicken Licken was about to follow when…all of a sudden, Goosey Loosey let out a loud "Honk!" Then Ducky Lucky let out a shrill "Quack!," and Cocky Locky cried out "Cock-a-doodle-doo!"

"Oh no!" cried Chicken Licken. "Foxy Loxy has eaten Goosey Loosey, Ducky Lucky, and Cocky Locky. I must run away!"

And she ran as fast as she could away from Foxy Loxy's den.

Chicken Licken ran all the way home without stopping. And she never did tell the king that the sky was falling down.

The Three Little Pigs

Once upon a time, there were three little pigs. Like all pigs, they loved to eat. But the more the three little pigs ate, the bigger they got. And the bigger they got, the more they ate. Soon, there was no room in their tiny house.

"It's no use," said their mother one morning. "You will have to leave home. You must go and build houses of your own."

So she packed their lunch in three handkerchiefs, and sent them on their way.

"Watch out for the big bad wolf," she warned, as she waved goodbye.

The three little pigs trotted off down the road. After a while, they met a man carrying bundles of straw.

"Excuse me, Sir," called the first little pig. "Please may I have some straw to build a house?"

"Of course," said the man, and he gave the little pig a bundle of straw.

The first little pig set to work, building his house. It was a tricky job, because the straw kept blowing away. But he never gave up. He worked long and hard all morning, until finally the house of straw was finished.

The two other little pigs continued down the road. It wasn't long before they met a farmer stacking sticks.

"Good morning!" cried the second little pig. "Please may I have some sticks to build a house?"

"Help yourself," replied the kind farmer. "There are plenty here."

So the second little pig set to work right away. It wasn't easy building a house of sticks, because it kept falling down. But she wouldn't give up either. She kept working all day long, until at last the house of sticks stayed up.

The third little pig continued down the road on his own, until he met a man pulling a cart of bricks.

"Bricks! What luck!" cried the third little pig, who was very smart. "Would you let me have some to build a house?"

"Take as many as you need," answered the kind man. "You are welcome to them."

The third little pig set to work on his house at once. The bricks were dusty and heavy, so it was very tiring. But he didn't stop for a moment. He worked hard all day, and all night, too, until finally the fine strong house of bricks was finished.

The next morning, the first little pig was sitting outside his straw house when the wolf came down his path. Quick as a flash, the little pig ran indoors and slammed the door shut.

"Little pig, little pig, let me in," growled the wolf, peering through the window.

"Not by the hairs on my chinny chin chin!" replied the frightened little pig.

"Then I'll huff and I'll puff and I'll blow your house down!" laughed the wolf.

And that's exactly what he did. With just one puff, the house of straw was no more.

"Help!" squealed the first little pig. Then he ran down the road to his sister's stick house as fast as he could.

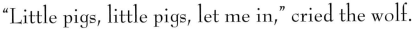

It wasn't long before the wolf arrived at the house of sticks. When the two little pigs saw him coming, they bolted the door and hid behind the sofa.

"Little pigs, little pigs, let me in," cried the wolf.

"Not by the hairs on our chinny chin chins!" cried the two little pigs. "Go away!"

"Then I'll huff and I'll puff and I'll blow your house down!" he said. So he huffed, and he puffed and down went the house of sticks.

"Oh my!" cried the two little pigs. They raced down the road to their brother's brick house, squealing all the way.

The third little pig was making a fire in his kitchen when he heard the commotion.

"Goodness!" he exclaimed, looking out of the window. He opened the front door to let his brother and sister in. The wolf wasn't far behind them, and he was looking very angry.

"Little pigs, little pigs, let me in," growled the wolf, banging on the door loudly.

"Not by the hairs on our chinny chin chins!" cried the three little pigs.

"Then I'll huff and I'll puff and I'll blow your house down!" roared the wolf. So he huffed and he puffed, he puffed and he huffed...but the fine strong house of bricks did not fall down. Not one little brick of it.

The wolf was furious.

"I'm coming down the chimney to gobble you all up!" he shouted to them loudly.

Now the third little pig was smart, and he knew exactly
what to do.

"Help me put this pot of water over the fire," he cried.

The three little pigs heaved the pot into place as the wolf
climbed onto the roof. Then they waited.

"Here I come," called the wolf, lowering himself into the
chimney.

WHOOSH! He slid down and landed with a SPLASH in the
pot of boiling water below.

"YOUCH!" he howled, leaping up into the air. And he raced
out of the kitchen as fast as his paws would carry him.

The three little pigs danced around the kitchen with delight.

"I don't think we'll see him again," they laughed. And they
were right. They didn't.

The Open Road

"Ratty," said Mole suddenly, one bright summer morning.
"I want to ask you a favour."

The Rat was sitting on the riverbank, singing a little song.

"Why, certainly," he said.

"Well, what I wanted to ask you is, can we call on Mr Toad? I've heard so much about him and would love to meet him."

"Get the boat out and we'll paddle up there at once, my friend. Toad is always in and will be delighted to meet you."

Rat and Mole rounded a bend in the river and came in sight of a handsome old stone house. Well-kept lawns reached down to the water's edge.

"There's Toad Hall," said Ratty. "Toad is rich and has the biggest house in these parts." They moored the boat in the boathouse and started to walk towards Toad Hall.

"Hooray!" cried Toad as the three animals shook paws.

"The very fellows I wanted to see! You've got to help me sort out something REALLY important!"

"It's about boating, I suppose?" asked the Rat, innocently.

"Forget about boating!" cried the Toad. "I've given that up LONG ago. Now I've discovered the REAL thing. Come with me and you will see!"

He led the way to the stable yard, where, in the open was a shiny new gypsy caravan painted green and canary yellow, with red wheels.

"There!" cried Toad. "There's the REAL life. A home from home, travelling the open road without a care in the world. Here today, somewhere else tomorrow."

The Mole, very interested and excited, followed Toad up the steps and inside. Ratty remained where he was, pretending to be uninterested, hands thrust deep in his pockets.

Inside the caravan were little sleeping bunks, a little table, a cooking stove, cupboards, bookshelves, and pictures of Toad on the walls.

"I've thought of everything," cried Toad. He pulled open a cupboard. "Here's everything WE could possibly want to eat." He threw open another cupboard. "Here's all the clothes WE could ever need, and spare pjyamas, washing things…everything! WE must start this very afternoon."

"I beg your pardon," said Rat's voice, from outside, "but did I hear you say something about WE?"

"Now, dear Ratty," said Toad, clambering down from the caravan. "Don't get on your high horse. You've just got to come; I can't possibly manage without you."

"I'm not coming and that's that," said the Rat. "I am going to stick to my boats and my dear old river. And what's more, Mole is going to stick with me, aren't you Mole?"

"Of course I am," said the Mole, loyally. "All the same…" he began hesitantly, "…it does sound as if it might have been fun."

"FUN! FUN! I'll say it would be fun," said Toad, and he began to paint the joys of caravanning in such glowing colours that the Mole could hardly stand still for excitement. In no time at all, it seemed, even the good-natured Rat had found himself interested in Toad's plans.

When it was agreed, the triumphant Toad led his friends to the paddock and asked them to capture the old workhorse. The horse hadn't been asked to drive the caravan and much preferred his paddock, so he made it difficult for Ratty and Mole to catch him.

At last the horse was caught and harnessed. And so it was that they set off, that afternoon after lunch, all three talking at once about what they would see on their travels. They ambled along dusty roads and beside orchards thick with cherry blossom.

Each animal took it in turns steering the caravan or walking either side of it. Tired and happy, and miles from home, they stopped for the night to eat supper before turning in to their little bunks in the caravan.

"This is the life, eh!" said a sleepy Toad. "Better than all your talk about your river, eh Ratty?"

"I *don't* talk about my river," replied the Rat. "You *know* I don't, Toad, but I *think* about it," he added quietly. "All the time." The Mole reached from under his blanket and gave Ratty's paw a squeeze. "Dear Ratty," he whispered. "Should we run away tomorrow morning and go back to our dear old hole on the river?"

"No, no, we'll see it out," whispered back the Rat. "We must stick by Toad until he's got over his caravanning craze. It won't take long. You'll see. Goodnight!"

The end was nearer than even the Rat suspected.

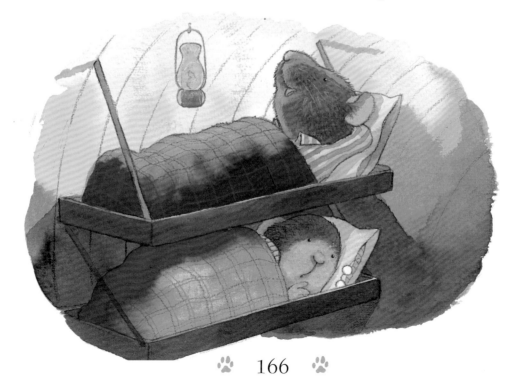

Next morning, Mole turned the horse's head onto their first really wide main road. Toad and the Rat were strolling behind when in the distance they heard a faint warning hum, like the drone of a distant bee. An instant later, with a loud "BEEP! BEEP!", a whirl of wind, and a BLAST of sound, a huge motor car tore past them.

The old horse let out a WHINNY of fear, reared, and plunged and bucked, and despite all Mole's efforts to control him, drove the caravan backward into a ditch, where it landed with a huge crash.

Ratty danced with rage. "You villains!" he shouted, shaking both fists. "You scoundrels, you…you…road hogs! I'll have the law on you!"

Mole, after successfully calming the horse, looked down at the caravan. It was a sad sight. Panels and windows were smashed, the axles hopelessly bent, one wheel off, and cans of food scattered across the shoulder of the road. And Toad? Toad sat, unmoving, in the middle of the road staring in the direction of the now disappeared car.

Every now and then, only faintly, he murmured "Beep-beep!"

The Rat shook him by the shoulder. "Come on Toad, do get up!"

But he wouldn't move.

"Glorious!" he murmured. "The poetry, the motion. That's the REAL way to travel. Here today – in next week tomorrow! Oh, bliss! Oh, beep-beep! Oh, my!"

"What are we to do with him?" asked the Mole.

"Oh, *drats* Toad!" said Ratty crossly. "I'm done with him! I've seen it all before. He's off onto a new craze. He'll be in a dream for days. We'll just have to get him to his feet, then make our way to the nearest town, and catch a train home."

"Now, look here, Toad!" said Ratty. "As soon as we get to the town, you'll have to go to the police station and make a complaint against that scoundrel and his car. Then you'll have to fix the wheels on the caravan."

"Police station! Complaint!" murmured Toad dreamily. "Me complain of that beautiful car? Oh Ratty, I might never have seen such a beautiful thing if it hadn't been for you agreeing to this trip."

The Rat shook his head in despair. He found a friendly farmer who would look after the old horse for the night. Then he, Mole, and Toad caught the next train back home.

It was a long, slow train ride home, but eventually they led a spellbound Toad to the doors of Toad Hall before rowing down river to the cosy warmth of Ratty's riverside home.

The following evening Mole was fishing from the riverbank when Ratty, who had been visiting friends, wandered up.

"Heard the news?" he asked. "There's nothing else being talked about. Toad went up to town this morning and ordered a large and very expensive car."

Ratty sighed. Some things would never change.

Mowgli and Baloo's Lessons

One day Bagheera, the black panther, was watching Baloo, the big brown bear, teach Mowgli the Law of the Jungle. There was so much to learn that Mowlgi started getting things wrong and Baloo cuffed him softly around the ears. Mowgli was so cross that he hid in the trees.

"He's so small," said the black panther. "How can you expect him to learn so much?" If it was up to Bagheera, he would have spoiled Mowgli.

"A man cub is a man cub, and he must learn all the Law of the Jungle," replied Baloo. "Nothing is too small to be killed. That's why I hit him, very softly."

"Softly, indeed, old Iron Fist," grunted Bagheera.

"Better he gets the odd pat from me than come to harm through ignorance," replied Baloo. "At the moment I'm teaching him the Master Words of the Jungle that will protect him from all the jungle creatures. Is that not worth a little cuffing? I'll call him and he will say them. Come, Little Brother."

Mowgli slid down a tree trunk and pulled a face at Baloo. "My head is ringing," he complained. "I come for Bagheera and not you, Baloo!"

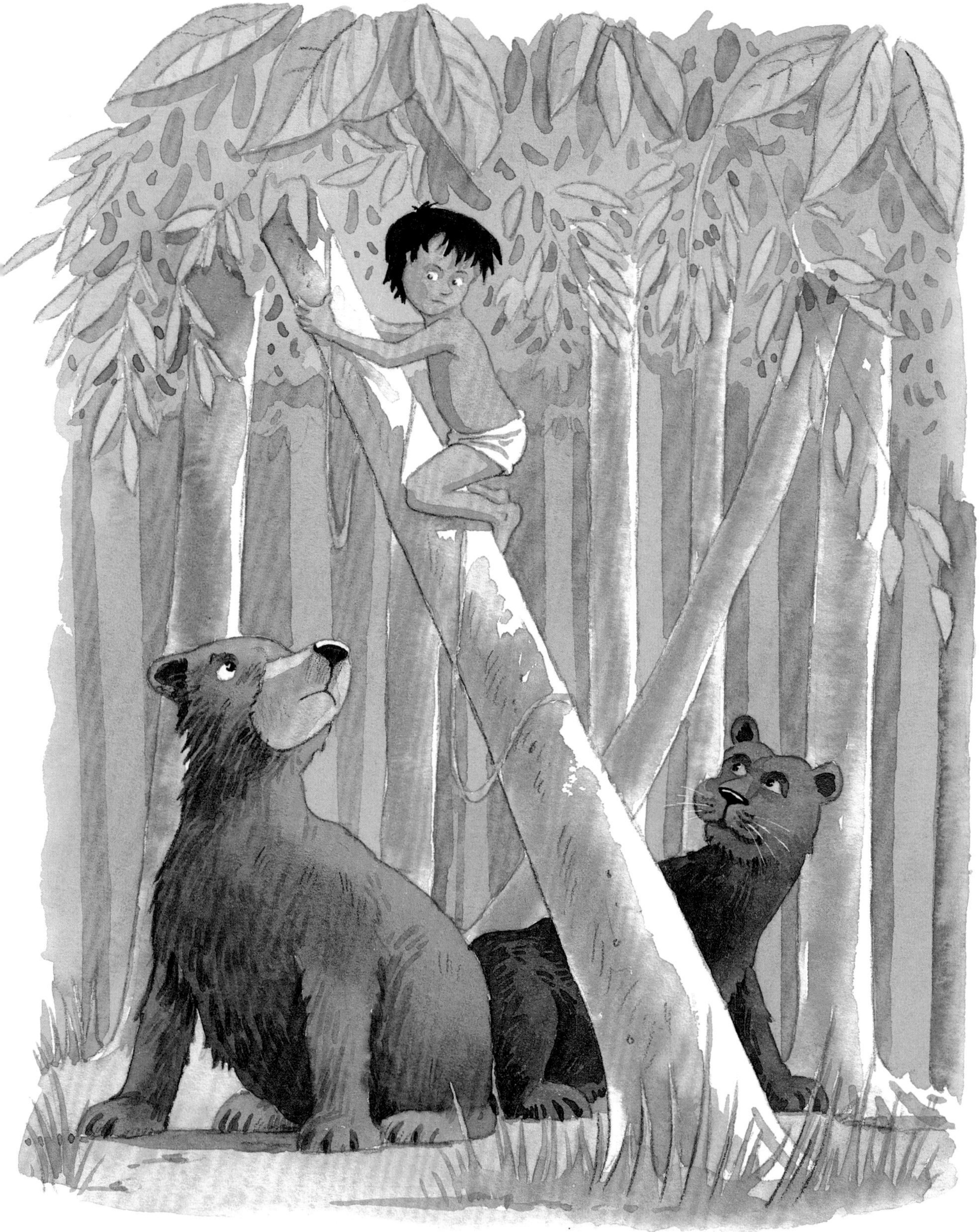

Baloo was a little upset by this because he loved the man cub. "Mowgli, why don't you tell Bagheera the Master Words of the Jungle?" said Baloo.

"Master Words for which people?" said Mowgli, who was delighted to show off. "The jungle has many tongues and I know them all." Then he rattled through the Words of the Animals, the Birds, and the Snakes. When he had finished he clapped his hands and pulled horrible faces at Baloo.

"One day I'll lead my own tribe through the branches. We'll throw branches and dirt at old Baloo," sang Mowgli.

"Mowgli," growled Baloo. "You've been talking with the Monkey People. They're evil."

Mowgli looked at Bagheera to see if the panther was angry, too, and Bagheera's face looked like cold ice.

"When you hurt my head, they came down and gave me nuts and said I should be their leader. No one else cared," he sniffed.

"They have no leader! They lie," said Bagheera.

"Well, I like them. They play all day," pouted Mowgli.

"Listen," said the bear, and his voice rumbled like thunder. "They have no Law. They creep around and spy. They boast and chatter and pretend to be great when they are not. We of the jungle ignore them even if they throw nuts and dirt at our heads.

As he spoke, a shower of nuts and twigs rained down on them. The evil Monkey People howled and shrieked above. One of them had had a brilliant idea. He'd decided that Mowgli would be a useful person to have in their tribe. He could teach them how to make huts like the ones humans lived in. With Mowgli's help, they would become the wisest people in the jungle.

The Monkey People waited until Baloo, Bagheera, and Mowgli were asleep, then they grabbed the little boy and swung him through the treetops.

Mowgli felt sick and giddy as they bounded, crashed, and whooped from one tree to the next. He knew that he had to get word back to his friends, for at the speed they were going Baloo and Bagheera would never be able to keep up. Mowgli saw Chil, the kite bird, circling above and remembered Baloo's lessons.

"We be of one blood, you and I," he called. "Tell Baloo and Bagheera that Mowgli passed this way."

Meanwhile, Baloo and Bagheera, who had heard Mowgli's cries, followed slowly below. Before too long, they came across Kaa, the python.

"What are you hunting?" hissed the snake.

"Monkey People, who have snatched Mowgli," explained Baloo.

"Ah, chattering, vain foolish things," hissed Kaa. "I'll help you hunt them."

Just then, there was a shout from above. "Look up, Baloo," called a voice. It was Chil, the kite. "Mowgli told me to tell you that the Monkey People have taken him to their city."

"Thank you, thank you," cried Baloo.

"It's no trouble," replied Chil. "The boy held the Master Words." Baloo's chest swelled with pride. Mowgli had remembered his lessons.

"Come," said Bagheera. "We must go to the Monkey People's city." And off raced Bagheera and Kaa, while Baloo trundled along behind.

Meanwhile, the Monkey People had arrived in the ruined city they called home. As they gathered around Mowgli, chattering about how great and wonderful they were, Mowgli began to think that they were all mad. He was wondering how he could escape when Bagheera raced down the hill and began knocking monkeys left and right. But there were too many and soon the brave panther was fighting for his life.

"Roll to the water tank," cried Mowgli. "They won't follow you there."

With a burst of strength, Bagheera threw off his attackers and lunged into the water tank. Just at that moment, Baloo lumbered in and took up the fight. Then Kaa pounced, eager and ready to kill.

Kaa was everything the monkeys feared. None could survive his deadly hug. With one hiss, the monkeys scattered with cries of "It is Kaa, run, run!"

Mowgli was free from the clutches of the terrible Monkey People. And after that day, he always, always tried his best to remember everything Baloo taught him.

The Musicians of Bremen

Once upon a time, a farmer had a donkey which had worked hard for him for many long years. But now the poor animal was old and unfit and the farmer wanted to get rid of him. However, before he could, the donkey (who was a very wise beast) decided to run away and become a musician.

The donkey set off for the town of Bremen, but before he'd walked far, he found a dog lying on the road. The dog was panting and gasping to get his breath.

"Why are you panting so hard, my friend?" asked the donkey.

"Ah," puffed the hound. "As I'm so old and weak and can no longer hunt, my master wanted to get rid of me, so I ran away. But how can an old mutt like me earn a living?"

"Hey, why don't you join me?" said the donkey. "I'm going to Bremen to become a musician."

The old dog quickly agreed, and they went on together.

After they had walked a short distance, they heard a cat meowing sorrowfully. It was sitting on the path with its tail drooped and its head hung low.

"Oh dear," said the donkey. "What's wrong with you? You look very sad."

"You'd be sad if your life was in danger. Because I'm old and toothless, and I prefer to lie beside the fire, instead of hunting for mice, my mistress wanted to get rid of me, so I ran away. But what am I going to do now?"

"Come with us to Bremen. You sing beautifully and will make a fine musician." The cat thought it sounded like a splendid idea and decided to join them.

They set off down the road, where they soon met a cockerel, who was crowing with all his might. "COCK-A-DOODLE-DOO!"

"Wonderful," cried the donkey. "You do make a splendid noise. But what's it all about?"

"My mistress has threatened to wring my neck and feed me to her guests on Sunday," replied the cockerel. "Now I'm crowing while I still can."

"We can't let that happen," said the donkey. "You'd better come with us. We're off to town to become musicians. If you can crow a bit more quietly, you could sing with us."

The cockerel quickly agreed, and all four carried on down the road.

That evening, the donkey and dog settled down beneath a tree. The cat settled on a low branch. And the cockerel flew to the top of the tree, where it was safest. Before settling down, the cockerel looked around and saw a light in the distance.

"There's a house not far from here," he called to his new friends. "I can see lights."

"In that case we'd better go on. It's sure to be warmer than here," said the donkey.

"Excellent idea," said the dog, licking his lips. He was hoping that there might be a bone or scrap to nibble on.

So they made their way through the trees until they came across a house, glowing with lights.

The donkey, being the biggest, went to the window and peered in first.

"What do you see?" asked the cockerel.

"A table covered with good things to eat and drink, and thieves sitting around enjoying themselves."

"This would be a perfect place for us to live," said the cockerel. And they all gathered around to talk. Before long, they came up with a plan for getting rid of the robbers.

The donkey stood on his hind legs and placed his front hooves on the window ledge. The dog jumped on his back. The cat climbed on the dog's back. And, last of all, the cockerel perched upon the cat's head. Then they began to perform their music:

"EEEE-OWWW! EEEE-OWWW!" the donkey brayed.

"WOOF! WOOF!" the dog barked.

"MEOW! MEOW!" the cat mewed.

"COCK-A-DOODLE-DOO!" the cockerel crowed.

Then they all burst in through the window, shattering the glass and scattering the robbers in all directions. The thieves, who thought that some horrible monster had come for them, scampered away as fast as they could.

The four animals sat down at the thieves' table and ate, and ate, and ate.

Then they turned out
the lights and searched for
a bed. The donkey lay down
on some straw in the yard.

The dog lay on the mat
beside the door.

The cat curled up in
front of the fire.

And the cockerel perched on top of the
chimney. After such a long and exciting
day, they all fell swiftly to sleep.

But they wouldn't have slept so quickly if they'd known that the thieves hadn't gone far. As soon as the thieves saw that the house was dark, they decided that they had been silly to run away and the bravest was sent back to investigate.

When the thief found the house so still and quiet, he went into the kitchen to light a candle. When he saw the fiery eyes of the cat glittering in the fireplace, he thought they were live coals and held some paper to them to get a light. The cat was furious. She flew at his face, spitting and scratching.

The thief was so scared that he ran for the door but the dog, who lay there, sprang up and bit his leg. The injured thief raced across the yard, where the donkey kicked him smartly on his backside.

Then the cockerel, who had been awakened by the noise, crowed, "COCK-A-DOODLE-DOO," with all his might.

The terrified thief ran away from the house as fast as he could to join the other thieves.

"There's a terrible witch in the house," he told his friends. "She spat at me and scratched my face with her long claws. Then there was a man by the door who stabbed me in the leg with a knife. And a monster in the yard who beat me with a wooden club. And on the roof there's a demon judge, who called out, 'COOK THE CROOK DO'. So I ran away while I still could."

After that night, the robbers never again dared to return to the house. And it suited the four musicians so well that they decided to stay. I expect that they are still there now.